This book should be returned to any branch of the
Lancashire County Library on or before the date shown

For Ivy Sienna Hart, special
first granddaughter for Pops,
with lots of love

Special thanks
to Sue Mongredien

ORCHARD BOOKS
338 Euston Road, London NW1 3BH
Orchard Books Australia
Level 17/207 Kent Street, Sydney, NSW 2000
A Paperback Original

First published in 2010 by Orchard Books

HiT entertainment

A CIP catalogue record for this book is available
from the British Library.

ISBN 978 1 40830 911 7

1 3 5 7 9 10 8 6 4 2

Printed in Great Britain

The paper and board used in this paperback are natural recyclable
products made from wood grown in sustainable forests. The
manufacturing processes conform to the environmental regulations
of the country of origin.

Orchard Books is a division of Hachette Children's Books,
an Hachette UK company

www.hachette.co.uk

Maisie
the Moonbeam Fairy

by Daisy Meadows

ORCHARD BOOKS

www.rainbowmagic.co.uk

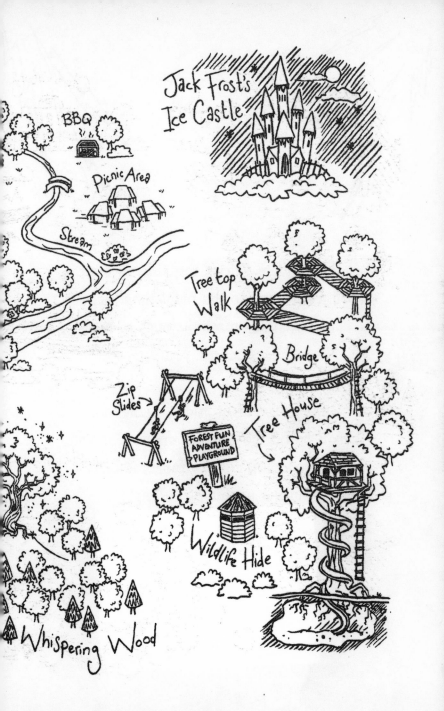

The Twilight Fairies' magical powers
Bring harmony to the night-time hours.
But now their magic belongs to me,
And I'll cause chaos, you shall see!

Sunset, moonlight and starlight too,
There'll be no more sweet dreams for you,
From evening dusk to morning light
I am the master of the night!

Contents

Mirror, Mirror

It was a cool, dark evening and Kirsty Tate and Rachel Walker were standing with a group of children at the side of Mirror Lake – a wide, still expanse of water surrounded by hills. The two friends were staying with their families at a holiday park called Camp Stargaze and were having a wonderful week so far.

As its name suggested, Camp Stargaze was the perfect spot to see the night sky in all its glory, and there were lots of unusual and exciting activities for the campers to do every night. So far, Kirsty and Rachel had been to a campfire midnight feast, had gone firefly-spotting in Whispering Wood, and had studied the stars from the Camp's observatory… and tonight they were about to set sail for a moonlit boat ride!

"Come on then, you landlubbers,"

called Peter, the camp leader. He led them along a small wooden jetty, and Kirsty and Rachel saw that a motorboat was tied up there. "All aboard, me hearties!"

Chattering and laughing, the children clambered aboard. The boat was lit with lanterns, which sent golden reflections into the dark water of the lake. The boat rocked gently as people took their seats, and Kirsty squeezed Rachel's hand excitedly once they'd sat down. "Every time I go on a boat it reminds me of the first time we met," she said. "Do you remember?"

Rachel smiled at her. The two girls had met on a ferry one summer when their families were both going on holiday to Rainspell Island. Kirsty and Rachel had liked one another immediately, and had gone on to have the most amazingly magical time together that week – and lots more adventures ever since!

"Of course I remember," Rachel replied.

"And I hope—" She broke off as Lucas and Matt, two boys that they'd made friends with, sat down nearby. The girls knew that they mustn't let anyone find out their secret: that they were friends with the fairies, and were often called to Fairyland, to help on important missions!

Kirsty could guess what Rachel had been about to say: that

 she hoped they had another fairy adventure that night! "I hope so too," she whispered quickly. The girls had been helping the Twilight Fairies search for their stolen bags of magic dust all week, but there were still two bags they hadn't managed to track down yet.

"Everyone ready? Then let's go!" called Peter just then. A lady called Alison started the engine of the boat, and its loud chugging broke the evening's quietness. Then the boat moved slowly away from the jetty and across the dark water.

"This lake is called Mirror Lake," Peter told everyone, "because in the daytime,

the water is usually so smooth and calm, it's like looking in a mirror. The moon is meant to be pretty full tonight, so I hoped we'd get a wonderful reflection in the water, but unfortunately it's rather cloudy." He shrugged.

"Hopefully the clouds will disappear soon, and the moon will come out. It looks amazing when it's reflected in the lake – twice as bright as usual!"

It didn't take long for the boat to reach the other side of the lake, where Alison and Peter tied it up to a second jetty, then helped everyone ashore. "Wow, look at these rocks," Matt said, shining his torch on them.

"They're really glittery, aren't they?"

"I think they're granite," Rachel said, switching on her torch so that she could see better. Kirsty fumbled in her pockets for her torch but couldn't find it.

"That's weird," she muttered to herself.
"I'm sure I had it earlier."

"Okay, listen up," Peter called.
"Tonight's activity is sending Morse Code
signals! If you didn't know, Morse Code is
a way of communicating with someone
else using short and long signals which
represent letters of the alphabet. I'll split
you into two teams, and you'll each have
a lamp to use for signalling to each other
across the lake, plus a copy of the Morse
Code alphabet."

Rachel and Kirsty
beamed at each
other. This sounded
fun!

"Rachel, Kirsty,
Lucas, Matt – you can
be one team," Peter went on.

"I'll take you to your base, further along the shoreline."

"And Hannah, Holly, Tom and Ben, you're in the second team," Alison said. "Follow me, guys, and we'll go in the opposite direction."

Alison's team struck out around the lake path, while Peter's team set off a different way. After a few minutes, Peter stopped walking and stared up at one of the hills. "That light isn't usually up there," he said, sounding puzzled. "Some people must be camping there, I guess."

Rachel and Kirsty turned their heads and gazed up to see what he meant. Beaming down from the nearest hill-top was a large light which was so bright and powerful, it made them both blink and look away.

"I hope that doesn't get much brighter," Peter said. "It could disturb the wildlife." He shrugged. "Hopefully they'll turn it off soon."

They continued walking around the lake until they reached an area where the path widened, and some logs had been arranged in a semi-circle. "Here we are," Peter said, setting the lantern on a flat rock overlooking the lake.

Just then they saw a flash of light from across the water, then another, then another. "Aha!" he said. "Perfect timing. That's the other team letting us know they're ready to start. Let's get ourselves all ready, then I'll signal back to them."

Peter gave Rachel the Morse Code sheet to hold, and Kirsty a notepad and pen, and the four children sat down on the logs. "OK," said Peter, and clicked the lantern on and off quickly three times. "They know we're ready too now, so keep a close watch and let's see if we can crack their code!"

Flashing Lights

They didn't have long to wait before the light across the lake started flashing. First there came a long flash, then a short one, then another long flash, and another short one. Then all was dark once more.

"So that was long, short, long, short," Peter said. "Can you find that on the alphabet sheet?"

Kirsty, Rachel and the boys pored over the chart. Each letter had a sequence of dots and dashes next to it. The dots represented short flashes of light, and the dashes stood for long flashes, Peter explained. "So you're looking for dash, dot, dash, dot," he said.

"There it is," said sharp-eyed Kirsty. "The letter C!"

"Well done, and just in time," Peter chuckled. "Here they go again!"

They sat in silence while the light across the lake flashed again – one short flash, then a longer one.

"Dot, dash," Matt said. "Easy – that's 'A'!"

There was a pause and then the third letter came. This was a long flash, then a short one, which represented the letter 'N'.

It was great fun deciphering the code. After several minutes they had got a few words: 'CAN YOU HEAR THE...'

The next letter was five long flashes.

"O," Lucas said, consulting the chart. Then came a short flash, followed by two long ones.

"W," said Kirsty and grinned. "'Can you hear the OW?' Do you think someone's hurt themselves over there?" she joked.

The final letter was a short flash, a long flash, and then two short flashes. "That's got to be 'L', surely," Rachel said, running her finger down the chart. "Yes – it is! So their message is 'Can you hear the owl?' Let's listen!"

Right on cue, they heard an owl hoot in the stillness of the night, and they all cheered and laughed.

"It's your turn to send a message back now," Peter said. "What do you want to say?"

Kirsty tried to think of something funny but was distracted by the nearby light on the hill top. "I'm sure that's getting brighter," she said, pointing up at it. "I know, why don't we send the others a message about it? We could ask them

if they know what's causing such a bright light."

"Good idea," Matt said. Between them, they spelled out 'WHAT DO YOU THINK THAT LIGHT IS?'

There was a pause, and then the other team spelled back, 'WE DON'T KNOW!'

"I can't help wondering," Kirsty hissed
to Rachel as Lucas, Matt and Peter
deciphered the last few letters, "if that
bright light has got something to do with
Jack Frost and the goblins. They've caused
so much night-time

trouble this week,
haven't they?"
Rachel
nodded. It
was true that
Jack Frost
had been up
to his tricks again.
He and his sneaky goblins had stolen
the bags of magic dust that the Twilight
Fairies used to keep everything running
smoothly throughout Fairyland and the
human world between dusk and sunrise.

Since the bags of dust had been taken,
things hadn't been happening as normal
– the sunset had been very late one
night, for example, the stars had changed
position in the sky, and the midnight feast
had almost been a disaster.

Kirsty and Rachel had helped five of
the seven Twilight Fairies find their bags
of magic dust now, but they really wanted
to find the last two bags before their
holiday was over.

Just then they heard a blood-curdling
shout. "Help! Help! We're lost in the
dark!"

Who's There?

Everyone gasped in shock. "Who said that?" Peter called, shining his torch into the shadows.

"It sounded as if it was coming from that direction," Lucas said, pointing at a cluster of granite boulders nearby. "Come on!"

They ran towards the boulders, which glittered as the torchlights fell on their surfaces. They searched behind them, then shouted into the woods beyond, and up the mountainside, but there was no reply – and no sign of anyone at all.

"How strange," Peter said, frowning. "Let's signal to the others, to see if they've heard any strange shouts this evening."

They wandered back to their signalling area… but the signal lamp had vanished!

"Where is it?" Matt cried, hunting for it around the rock it had been on. "Do you think it fell in the lake?"

Peter shook his head. "We'd have heard the splash if it did," he reasoned. "And it couldn't have fallen in – there's no breeze at all."

"Then where is it?" Lucas asked. "Is someone playing a trick on us, do you think?"

Nobody answered, but just then, Kirsty remembered her missing torch and had the horrible feeling that Lucas might be right. Perhaps someone *was* playing a trick... and perhaps that someone was a goblin!

Rachel nudged Kirsty. "Look – over there!" she hissed. "Is it me, or is that granite boulder glittering all by itself?"

31

Kirsty stared. Yes – one corner of a rock was sparkling very brightly. "That looks like fairy magic," she whispered excitedly. "Come on, let's take a closer look."

She and Rachel tiptoed away from Peter and the boys back to the rocky area, where one of the rocks was still glittering and twinkling. As they got nearer, they saw to their delight that a tiny fairy was perched on the rock, her wings sparkling against the dark sky. "It's Maisie!" Rachel said, hurrying over. "Hello again!"

Maisie was one of the Twilight Fairies, who used her special magic to look after the moon and its moonbeams. She had long, corn-coloured hair that was rolled up in a chignon, and wore a midnight blue dress with a pink frill at the bottom,  as well as a chunky, sparkly cardigan, and a crescent-moon pendant around her neck.

Maisie fluttered over to Kirsty and Rachel as soon as she saw them approaching, and hovered in mid-air.

"Hello," she said in a sweet, silvery voice. "I was hoping you'd notice me. I didn't dare come any closer with those boys around, but I've seen everything that's been going on."

"Seen everything? So do you know what happened to our lamp?" Kirsty asked her.

Maisie nodded. "There were a couple of goblins hiding nearby," she replied. "One

of them called out, pretending to need help and then, when you all rushed over, he and his friend took your lamp and ran off with it."

"I knew it must be goblins!" Kirsty burst out. "Which way did they go?"

"Up the hill," Maisie replied. "I'm sure they've got something to do with that bright light that's shining up there. I'm worried they're trying to interfere with the moon somehow, with the help of my magic moonbeam dust."

"Well, we'll help you," Rachel said at once. "Although…" Her eyes drifted back towards Peter, Matt and Lucas who were still hunting for the missing lamp. "They'll get worried if we disappear."

"Don't worry," Maisie reassured her. "I'll work some magic to make it seem as if you're only away from them for a second." She waved her wand in a swirling pattern, and hundreds of pink sparkles flooded out from it, twinkling in the darkness. "There," she said. "It'll only last a while, so there's no time to waste. I'll turn you both into fairies and we can fly up the hill to see what those sneaky goblins are up to!"

Moondust Magic

Maisie waved her wand again, and this time the sparkling fairy dust whirled all around Kirsty and Rachel. Moments later, a tingling sensation whizzed through their bodies and they felt themselves shrinking smaller and smaller, until they were the same size as Maisie, with colourful gleaming wings on their backs. They were fairies!

"Off we go," Maisie said, and she, Kirsty and Rachel all fluttered their wings and took off up the hill. It became much colder, the higher they flew, and the light from the top became stronger and brighter. As they neared the topmost point, the light was so powerful that they had to shield their eyes as they flew.

"Oh my goodness," Maisie exclaimed suddenly. She stopped flying and clapped a hand to her mouth, then fluttered up into the sky, not wanting to be seen.

Rachel and Kirsty who had been flying slightly behind her, flew up high too, then peered out to see what had surprised Maisie. There they saw a group of goblins... and the most extraordinary creation. Using sticks, pieces of wood, string, an old chair and pieces of litter, the goblins had assembled a large disc, on which was tied all sorts of torches, lanterns, lights, glow sticks and even glow-in-the-dark stickers!

Many of the lights were running from a
portable electricity generator which was
marked 'Property of Camp Stargaze'.
They'd obviously stolen *that* as well.

"I don't understand," Rachel said,
confused. "What are they doing?"

"I think," said Maisie hesitantly, "that
they're trying to make a moon."

"Make a *moon*?" Kirsty echoed. "But…
but nobody can make a
moon!"

"Well, we know that,"
Maisie replied, "but
obviously nobody's ever
told them." Then she
stiffened, as they saw
one of the goblins holding
a small blue satin bag that was tied with
a drawstring.

The goblin opened the bag, plunged his knobbly green fingers inside, then pulled out a pinch of glittering white dust and sprinkled it over the rigged-up 'moon'.

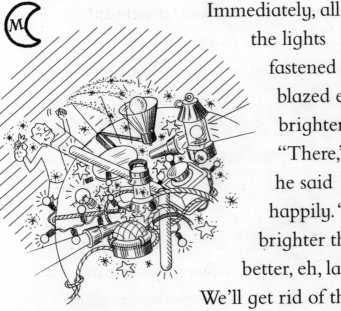

Immediately, all the lights fastened to it blazed even brighter. "There," he said happily. "The brighter the better, eh, lads? We'll get rid of the darkness with our lovely moon."

"That's my bag," Maisie said tensely. "And that's my moondust. We've got to get it back!"

Just then the girls and Maisie heard
heavy footsteps behind them, and the
unmistakable sound of goblin laughter.
They crouched low in the bush and
pulled its branches close around them

as two goblins tramped
past. "Look what we
got!" one of them
crowed.

Rachel, Kirsty
and Maisie saw
him holding up
the lamp that had
been stolen from the
Morse Code game. The other goblins
cheered. "Good work!" one called. "Let's
get it tied to our moon at once."

They lashed the lamp onto the disc with
a length of twine, humming cheerfully.

"Jack Frost is going to be so pleased with us," one of them commented. "He's going to love this moon."

"Yeah, and we'll make it bigger and bigger, and brighter and brighter, so it's like a full moon, every night," another boasted. "Unlike the other, silly moon which hardly ever shines brightly."

"Darkness will be gone forever!" cheered the first goblin. "The goblins have conquered darkness!"

Maisie shook her head in disbelief. "No, no, *no*!" she sighed. "This is such a bad idea.

It could mean disaster for the whole of Fairyland!"

"What do you mean?" Kirsty whispered, feeling worried at Maisie's words.

"Well, sooner or later, someone will wonder where this bright light is coming from, and will climb up here to investigate," Maisie began explaining. "And then, when they find the goblins, the secret of Fairyland will be revealed. We can't let that happen!"

"No," Rachel agreed. "People from Camp Stargaze have already noticed. Peter, our leader, thought it was caused by campers, but if the light keeps shining night after night, and getting brighter and brighter, he'll want to investigate, I'm sure."

Kirsty pointed to the generator which was whirring loudly as it lit the goblins' moon. "Let's start by taking a closer look at that," she suggested. "If we can find the 'off' switch, we'll be able to put out some of their lights."

"Good idea," Maisie said. "Come on."

Very carefully and quietly, the three fairies ventured nearer the generator, keeping close to the ground and ducking behind stones and clumps of grass whenever they thought one of the goblins was about to look their way.

Then, just as they were approaching the generator, they saw a goblin put the bag of moondust down on the ground before leaning over the generator to adjust something.

"Even better," Maisie whispered. "I'll just fly over and grab my bag instead! Without my dust, their silly moon won't shine so brightly."

And she darted towards her bag, her hand outstretched. But just as she was about to take the bag, Rachel and Kirsty saw the goblin pull a large lever on the generator. The lever increased the power instantly, causing the 'moon' to shine even brighter.

Maisie almost jumped out of her skin as the light blazed down on her, and she fluttered up in panic.

"Hey!" shouted a goblin, pointing towards her. "There's a fairy! Someone catch it!"

49

Caught!

Before Maisie could escape, one of the goblins had thrust out a hand and grabbed her. "Lovely," he chortled, examining her. "You're nice and sparkly – just what we need for our moon." With his other hand he picked up a length of string and deftly tied her to the 'moon'. "There," he said with a satisfied grunt.

"Perfect. You can add to the brightness and, best of all, now you're there, you won't be able to interfere with our plans!"

"You're making a mistake," Maisie cried. "Please – let me go. Your moon isn't a good idea, because—"

But the goblins wouldn't let her finish. "Not a good idea? Our moon is a brilliant idea!" one of them told her. "You just look sparkly and keep quiet, all right?"

Kirsty and Rachel, who were hiding behind a stone, clung to one another nervously. They had to rescue their fairy friend – but how?

The goblins began attaching the stolen lamp to their moon but soon got into a heated argument about which was the best way to do it. "We've got to think of a plan," Kirsty whispered to Rachel. "We need to trick the goblins somehow. Let's see… What might tempt them?"

Rachel was finding it hard to think while the goblins bickered. "We need the lamp to go *here*, to make the moon brighter," one snapped, snatching it out of another's hands.

"No, you idiot, it'll be much better this side," another argued, grabbing it back.

Then Rachel smiled. It was obvious what the goblins wanted most of all! "More light," she suggested. "Anything to make their moon brighter!"

Kirsty nodded. "Of course," she agreed.

"So what would be the most dazzling light of all? What would they be desperate to have on their moon?"

Both girls fell silent as they thought. Then something Peter had said earlier came back to Rachel, about the moon's light seeming twice as strong as usual when it was reflected in Mirror Lake. "The real moon's reflection in the lake will be very bright, if it comes out from behind the clouds," she whispered. "We

could convince the goblins to try and catch its reflection!"

"That's a brilliant idea!" Kirsty replied. Then her face fell.

"But they'll never believe us if we're fairies – or even if Maisie magics us back into girls. They'll know we're trying to trick them."

"Then we'll just have to ask Maisie to disguise us," Rachel said, thinking quickly.

"As... as astronomers!"

"Perfect," Kirsty agreed. "If we look like astronomers, the goblins will think we're experts."

The goblins were still arguing loudly about where to put the lamp so Kirsty and Rachel fluttered over to Maisie and whispered their idea to her.

"Good thinking," Maisie smiled. "And don't worry about waiting for the moon to come out from the clouds – I'll use my magic to melt those clouds away."

Maisie's arms had been tied down so that she could hardly move them but she just managed to twirl her wand and mutter some magic words. Seconds later, Rachel and Kirsty were their usual size, and were wearing white coats and carrying telescopes. Their hair was tied back and they were also wearing glasses. Their hearts pounding, they strode in front of the goblins' moon and pretended to study it.

"Marvellous, marvellous," Rachel said loudly. "Quite incredible the way this has been put together."

The goblins stopped arguing and turned to see who was praising their creation.

"Splendid," Kirsty agreed, peering closely at the brightly-lit disc as if she were an expert. "Whoever made this is clearly very clever indeed. Very clever."

The goblins looked delighted at her words. "Well, yes, we *are* clever," they said happily. "We're very clever indeed!"

"Although..." Rachel frowned. "Speaking as an astronomer, I'd say that to ensure that the night is never dark again, this moon needs to be much brighter."

"Oh yes," Kirsty said. "Much more light is needed here. As a fellow astronomer, I completely agree."

The goblins stopped looking so smug and scratched their heads. "More light?"

one said meekly. "But we've pinched— I mean, we've collected every light we could find. Where can we get more light?"

Just at that moment, the clouds around the real moon slid clean away from it, revealing its pearly whiteness shining brightly down. And there in Mirror Lake was its mirror image, a full, round reflection which was every bit as bright as the real thing. Clever Maisie had worked her moon magic at exactly the right time!

"Down there, of course," Rachel said, pointing at the lake as if it were obvious.

"All you need to do is collect that reflection and your moon will be the best one around," Kirsty assured the goblins.

"No problemo!" one of them replied. "Come on, lads. To the lake!"

Moon in the Mirror

Off ran the goblins, taking the bag of moon dust with them, whooping and cheering with great excitement.

As soon as they were out of sight, Rachel and Kirsty untied Maisie who fluttered gratefully up into the air, shaking out her wings.

They switched off the generator, which made most of the lights go out, then Maisie turned the girls back into fairies, and they soared down the hillside towards Mirror Lake.

The goblins were splashing around in the shallows, moaning about their cold, wet feet as they tried to grab hold of the reflected moon. But of course, every time they lunged towards it, the water would ripple and the reflection would break up into silvery streaks.

"Those astronomers said we'd be able to catch it," moaned the goblin who had the bag of magic moondust. Then he glanced up towards their moon and gaped when he saw how weakly it was shining now. "Hey!" he shouted, throwing his hands up crossly…and accidentally letting go of the bag of moondust.

"Catch it!" Kirsty cried as the bag went flying over the lake. She, Rachel and Maisie all dived frantically to catch the bag…and just managed to grab it together before it hit the water.

They flew up high and Maisie shrank the bag back to its usual Fairyland size. The girls grinned – they'd done it!

Meanwhile, down below, the goblins all looked very disgruntled. "That's not fair," they moaned, stomping back to the shore. "You rotten fairies have spoiled our plan – again!"

"Sorry," Maisie said, "but I'll have to spoil your moon too, by returning all those lamps and lights you took. I know you worked hard on it, but none of those things were yours to use. One moon in the sky is plenty, I think! After all, it is important to have darkness some of the time."

The three fairies flew around the lake, away from the goblins, and Maisie turned Kirsty and Rachel back into girls. "Thank you *so* much," she smiled. "It's great to have my moon dust again. And now, if you follow the path that way, you'll soon be back with your friends."

She kissed the girls — light, delicate fairy kisses, that felt tickly and soft, and they all said goodbye. Rachel and Kirsty watched as she flew off into the dark sky, holding her special bag of dust very tightly.

Then they blinked as a familiar-looking lamp appeared at their feet – it was the one the goblins had taken from them earlier!

Kirsty picked it up and they followed the path around as Maisie had told them to. Seconds later, they saw Peter, Matt and Lucas, and gave a shout. "Look what we found!"

"Oh, well done!" Peter said. "Where was it?"

"Just down there," Rachel replied honestly. "Maybe somebody was playing a trick on us – but at least we've got the lamp back now."

"And I know just the message to send," Peter said with a grin. "Who can remember the signal for the letter 'H'?"

As the message went on, it soon became clear that Peter was spelling out 'HOT CHOCOLATE?' to the other team.

"Now you're talking!" Kirsty smiled, as he produced a large thermos flask and some cups.

The other team didn't need asking twice, and came around to join them. Then, as Peter poured out steaming mugfuls for everyone, he happened to glance up the hill. "Oh, look, the light's gone off up there," he said. "That's good – everything's back to normal now."

"It certainly is," Rachel said to Kirsty, and they exchanged a secret smile. Helping the Twilight Fairies was turning out to be such fun!

RAINBOW magic

The Twilight Fairies

Now Rachel and Kirsty have helped
Maisie, it's time to help...

Sabrina the Sweet Dreams Fairy

Nightmares!

"Oh, isn't it sad that this is our last night at Camp Stargaze, Kirsty?" Rachel sighed as she snuggled down inside her sleeping bag. She glanced up at the black velvet sky overhead, the tiny silvery stars glittering like diamonds. "Still, having an outdoor sleepover is a brilliant way to end the holiday!"

Kirsty nodded as she unzipped her own sleeping bag and climbed in. "It's been huge fun, hasn't it, Rachel?" she agreed. "I'm so glad we came!"

The girls and their parents were spending a week of the summer holidays at Camp Stargaze, which was so called because it was in a wonderful location to view the night sky. It was a warm, clear evening and all the children had brought their sleeping bags out onto the lawn beside the tents. They'd had juice and cookies, and Peter, the camp leader, had read them a bedtime story.

"OK, time to put your torches out now," Peter called. "Goodnight, everyone."

"I'd like to come back to Camp Stargaze again next year," said Lucas. He and Matt, two of Rachel and Kirsty's new friends, were lying on the lawn in their sleeping bags near the girls. "It's been the best holiday I've ever had!"

"I've learned a lot about the stars from Professor Hetty," Matt declared, switching off his torch. "And I'm going to carry on reading up about them when I get home, too. Goodnight, Rachel and Kirsty!"

"Goodnight," the girls called.

All the torches had been turned off now and the camp was in darkness except for the pale light of the moon. Gradually everything fell silent although the girls could hear the occasional gentle hooting of an owl in the Whispering Wood nearby.

"No-one else knows that this has been an extra-magical holiday for us, Kirsty," Rachel whispered, smiling at her friend in the moonlight.

"Yes, we've had some amazing fairy

adventures!" Kirsty whispered back.

When the girls had arrived at Camp
Stargaze, their fairy friends had asked
for their help once more. Rachel and
Kirsty had been horrified to learn that
Jack Frost and his goblins had stolen
seven satin bags of magical dust from the
Twilight Fairies while the fairies were at
their own outdoor party. The Twilight
Fairies used their magic to make sure
that the hours between dusk and dawn
ran smoothly and were peaceful and
harmonious, just as they should be. But
with the magic bags in the hands of Jack
Frost and his goblins, all sorts of strange
things had been happening, including a
green sunset and the stars moving around
in the sky!

"I know we've found six of the bags,"

Rachel said, "But there's still one fairy left to help - Sabrina the Sweet Dreams Fairy."

Rachel, Kirsty and the Twilight Fairies had been determined to find the bags of magical dust after Jack Frost's icy magic had sent his goblins spinning away to the human world to hide the bags there. So far the girls and the fairies had managed to outwit the goblins time and time again and retrieve almost all of the bags.

"Let's hope we can find Sabrina's bag tomorrow before we go home," Kirsty said with a yawn. "Goodnight, Rachel."

"Goodnight, Kirsty," Rachel replied.

A few moments later, Kirsty heard her friend breathing deeply and knew she was asleep. Kirsty cuddled down in her sleeping-bag, feeling comfortably warm and drowsy. She gazed up at the sky,

but suddenly she noticed that the light of
the moon had vanished. For a moment
Kirsty thought the moon had slipped
behind a cloud, but then it re-appeared
for a second or two before disappearing
again. It was almost like someone was
flipping a switch and turning the moon
on and off, Kirsty thought, puzzled.

Then she saw that the stars were
moving. They were whizzing around
the night sky, mixing up all of the
constellations, and making Kirsty dizzy
just to watch them.

Suddenly Kirsty heard a cold, icy
chuckle very close by that sent a shiver
down her spine.

"Ha ha ha! Those silly girls and their
pesky fairy friends are no match for me
this time!" Jack Frost gloated. "I have

ALL the Twilight Fairies magical bags,
and now I am the master of the night-
time hours!"

"Hurrah for Jack Frost!" the goblins
cheered.

"No!" Kirsty gasped. "This can't be
happening..."

Suddenly Kirsty jerked herself awake.
She was all hot and flustered and tangled
up in her sleeping-bag.

"Oh, I was dreaming!" Kirsty sighed
with relief. "I didn't even realise I'd fallen
asleep. What a horrible nightmare!"
She glanced across at Rachel and was
surprised to see her friend sitting up,
yawning and pushing her hair out of her
eyes.

"Are you OK, Kirsty?" Rachel asked.
"I just had a terrible dream about Jack

Frost and the goblins..."
"Oh, so did I!" Kirsty exclaimed, and
quickly she told Rachel about her dream.
  "My nightmare was that Jack Frost
kidnapped all the Twilight Fairies and
imprisoned them in his Ice Castle,"
Rachel said with a sigh. "It seemed
so real..."

Read the rest of
Sabrina
the Sweet dreams Fairy

to find out what magic happens next...

Available now!

The Twilight Fairies

Win Rainbow Magic goodies!

In every book in the Twilight Fairies series
(books 92-98) there is a hidden picture of a moon with a
letter in it. Find all seven letters and re-arrange them to
make a special Twilight Fairies word, then send it to us.
Each month we will put the entries into a draw and select
one winner to receive a Rainbow Magic sparkly T-shirt
and goody bag!

Send your entry on a postcard to Rainbow Magic
Twilight Fairies Competition, Orchard Books, 338 Euston
Road, London NW1 3BH. Australian readers should write
to Hachette Children's Books, Level 17/207 Kent Street,
Sydney, NSW 2000.
New Zealand readers should write to Rainbow Magic
Competition, 4 Whetu Place, Mairangi Bay, Auckland,
NZ. Don't forget to include your name and address.
Only one entry per child.
Final draw: 30th September 2011.

Have you checked out the

website at:
www.rainbowmagicbooks.co.uk

Meet the Showtime Fairies

in April 2011!

Madison the Magic Show Fairy
978-1-40831-286-5

Leah the Theatre Fairy
978-1-40831-287-2

Alesha the Acrobat Fairy
978-1-40831-288-9

Darcey the Dance Diva Fairy
978-1-40831-289-6

Taylor the Talent Show Fairy
978-1-40831-290-2

Amelia the Singing Fairy
978-1-40831-291-9

Isla the Ice Star Fairy
978-1-40831-292-6